Joseph H. Armstrong

Lyrics, Idyls and Fragments

Joseph H. Armstrong

Lyrics, Idyls and Fragments

ISBN/EAN: 9783744788403

Printed in Europe, USA, Canada, Australia, Japan

Cover: Foto ©Andreas Hilbeck / pixelio.de

More available books at **www.hansebooks.com**

LYRICS, IDYLS

AND

FRAGMENTS

BY

JOSEPH H. ARMSTRONG

"I reap the red tares that I sow not,
And sow—as I cannot reap."

"My heart is but a purple song unsung,
Save in the pathos of a minor part
Whose sweeter chords are clogged with aching clay."

J. H. A.

NEW YORK
THE PUBLISHERS' PRINTING COMPANY
Nos. 120 AND 122 EAST 14TH STREET
1892

INDEX.

4

5

TO THE READER.

T O edit this little book of verses has been no easy
task. It soon became evident that an unbiased
criticism was impossible. There was ever present
the sympathy of friendship, which either attracted
unduly or, when checked, became the cause of undue
severity of judgment. Hence I limited myself to a
presentation of such poems as seemed likely to claim
the favor of some reader, though not setting forth all
that subsists of the fragmentary work of the poet.
Pieces which it is more than likely that a few addi-
tional years of life would have cancelled are never-
theless presented, for the sake of some lines here
and there, perhaps some stanzas, which must have
been saved from such a doom, and incorporated
into poems yet unconceived and now never to be
conceived.

Is it the true part of a friend to put immature
work into the world's show-windows of poetic reading? Because Kirke White died at twenty-one, shall

generation after generation be haunted by his gaunt ghost of would-be poetry? We pity the fate of an ardent student, but we cannot commend, because of our sympathy, his lifeless verse.

Stood the case so, in my opinion, with the work of my friend, I should have recommended the destruction of all that he had written, for his own sake rather than for the world's. But I believe that nobody can read "The Serenade," "Life and I were Ill at Ease," "Florida," or the rondel "On a Woman's Eyes," without being attracted, nay, more or less fascinated. The light step, the fling and careless pathetic grace bring to mind the songsters of cavalier days.

Then "An Answer to a Proposal" is a piece possessing indubitable excellence in its way—that, in company with its less reckless but more mutinously sweet sister, "Chant de Nuit," bids fair, unless my mind is utterly misled by friendship, to rival, with poetic readers, some of the very best poems of the kind now extant.

But apart from such fragrant work as "The Shower" and others of the sort, there is lyric work of a more serious character, and deserving, I think, far higher praise. "The Glow-worm," while Browning-haunted, is still his own, and an impressive piece of verse. It is compactly done, and reveals beauties to a second and third reading. "Ergo

Sum " is a little masterpiece, and combines serious questionings with exquisite loveliness and delicate irony. The stanzas "The Unseen Singer" are, of all his work, the noblest. As the poet listens to the voice and wonders what face, attitude, and glory of soul may belong to the singer, he reads the great lesson of faith. God is the unseen singer who chants in nature, whose sweetest tones ring in the heart itself, and, longing to hear more distinctly, to catch a glimpse of the unimaginable face, man has become what he is—has become God-like. Then the painful verses that contrast lethargy of spirit with peace, ending in a pious breathing of adoring praise! Such a lyric is not the· product of a rhymer, of an immature heart and brain, but is an artist's—a true poet's child.

Among the lyrics is a fragment entitled "Sanity." This piece of close-knit blank verse will be found repeated, in somewhat altered form, in the body of one of the tales. It was found in this separate form, and since in this separateness it speaks more personally, it appears where it does, as well as in the "Suicide."

To draw attention to the fact that Mr. Armstrong was a writer according to two entirely different methods may serve to explain the inspirationalism evident in many of his lyrics, and the careful medi-tated style of other samples of his workmanship. If

9

"Timoleon's Love," for instance, had no further merit than its self-restrained manner and its excellently developed metaphors, which are, after the example of Elizabethan dramatists, worked out into detail, it would, in my opinion, deserve publication.

> . . . "As the sun went down,
> Stripping of all their purple uniform
> His soldiery of clouds, until they looked
> Quite woe-begone, like self-stung renegades
> That had gone over to advancing night,"

is a fair example of his metaphors wrought into perfectness.

The idyls and tales speak for themselves. "Marco Miale" was found in a very disordered form. It was only after great pains that the thread of narrative was traced through the many fragments which were afterward arranged so as to produce the apparently intended effect; the poem had really never been written. Notes, as it were, had been jotted down at odd moments, some in pencil, some in ink; now overlapping in subject, now almost contradictory. For the arrangement of the poem, such as it is, the editor is responsible. Whatever is good belongs to the poet, whatever is marred must be set down to the ill judgment of his friend.

"Memories, a Study in E Minor," is an attractive poem, the suggestive sweetness and passion of which may possibly escape the reader at the first perusal.

It seems to me in some respects an example of his most finished work.

To be sure, like all young poets he was under the spell of master-singers, and echoes mingle with his own voice. And now all that remains to be done is to draw the reader's attention to the pronunciation of words like "trifling" and "rippling" in three syllables, "spiritual" in two, and such words as "heaven," "rhythm," "chasm," "flower," "fire," and "hour" as dissyllables.

It is hoped that this little volume may add a few fragrant blossoms to the Southern nosegay, and in some measure win for the unfortunate poet the recognition he dreamed of, as the well-earned crown of future work which weakness, disease, and death forbade.

NORMAN DE LAGUTRY.

TO J. H. A.

DEAR fellow-wanderer through enchanted days,
　　How the moon shone!
Dear fellow-chooser of unbeaten ways,
　　Were the flowers sweet?
Dear fellow-seeker after glories strange,
　　Was thy face thin and wan?
Ah! We are struggling thro' great seas of change,
　　And thou art set beyond all hope's defeat!

Nay, we can weep for what is lost alone,
　　But thou art near—
More near than ere from earth thy soul had flown
　　To sunlit hills.
For where I am, thither I summon up
　　Thy spirit from its sphere;
Thy hand holds to my lips a golden cup,
　　Whose sunny draught all ache of yearning stills.

Thou knowest all—I need to tell thee naught—
　　Thou knowest all.
Nor are we broken-hearted. Thou hast taught
　　To heed the call
Of spirit voices, and they cheer us on
　　To look for higher things;
The past was fair—but see the future's dawn!
　　And joy can reach it on his passion-wings.

N. DE L.

BIOGRAPHICAL SKETCH.

JOSEPH H. ARMSTRONG, the son of Richard F. Armstrong and grandson of the late Gen. James W. Armstrong, of Macon, Ga., was born in Halifax, N. S., on the nineteenth of September, 1867. An inherited delicacy of constitution, however, necessitated his removal to a warmer climate, and being of Southern parentage, he quickly and naturally identified himself with the people among whom the traditions of his family lay. Being debarred by frequent illnesses from participating in the rougher sports of boyhood, as well as from undertaking the irksome tasks of the school-room, his education proceeded in the desultory fashion natural where a quick and inquiring mind is left unrestrained in its pursuits; and in the ardor of study his tasks and his pleasures became often identical.

It was not until his eighteenth year that it was thought practicable to subject him to the demands and restrictions of a fixed course of study, the many advantages offered by the University of the South first suggesting such a possibility. At that institution he accordingly remained for three years—the value of which, in mental and physical training, as well as in that contact and association which is so needful a preparation for entrance upon active life, he fully and justly appreciated; while an entry in his journal at this time expresses the poignant regret with which the ties there formed were severed.

In the summer of 1889 he visited Halifax for a brief period, soon finding it imperative to return to the milder Southern air. Even in that favorable climate, however, an attack of *la grippe* developed the disease against which he had so long been guarded; and one more summer brought to its close the brief story of his life, his strength barely sufficing for a return to that land whose soft airs had so often restored him to comparative health. The winter of 1890–91 proved singularly unfavorable, provoking the lines entitled "Florida," the loving mockery of which is in one of his characteristic veins, and in which the pen falls from the weak hand in most pathetic confirmation of the arraignment.

St. Augustine had been always his best-loved home, with its relics of an older time, its vague associations of history and romance, its charm of sea and sky, and its free and informal yet refined social life; and it was in this chosen spot that, in January,

1891, after a month in which the patient and brave spirit seemed alone to sustain the sinking body, he passed away, retaining to the last conscious moment the vivacity and clearness of intellect which were characteristic of him.

As a student his love of poetry transcended all others, and though tempted by an ardent and somewhat mercurial temperament to try many departments of art, he ever returned to the old love; and his ambition, conceived at an age when few boys look beyond the play-ground, was ever for achievement in that field. His style, as is natural in youth, was much influenced by his enthusiasm for certain writers, though unconsciously so—Keats, perhaps, having made the earliest and hence the deepest impression; the hardening of fibre and assertion of individuality having just begun to be evident in his latest work.

In the restlessness of an ardent and aspiring mind, impatient of commonplace formulas, fascinated at times by the specious philosophies of the day, yet never satisfied with their conclusions, he struggled onward toward the light, finding a vantage-ground in that higher pantheism which seems not to be incompatible with the truth revealed to us. In " The Glow-worm" is a touch of this belief, and in his last verses, " The Unseen Singer," is shadowed the conflict which had at last reached its peaceful result.

To remind his friends, for whom this volume is primarily intended, of his many companionable qualities, of the keen and ready wit, the quaint humor, and the fine insight, would perhaps be needless, while to the sympathetic much of this will be discernible in his writings.

It is but just to remind the reader that the author of this book had lived but little over twenty-three years; that almost all was written before even that age had been attained, and that the greater part, written in moments of depression, in the weariness of sleepless nights, and often in the intervals of suffering, was thrown aside in the impatience of severe self-criticism, either to be destroyed or to await, for revisal, a future day of calmer judgment and maturer culture—a day to which all serious and sustained work was hopefully postponed, but which, alas! was never to be.

TO MY MOTHER.

THOUGH I be cast a plaything on the shore
    Of bleak despair by some wild storm of doubt,
Or stand upon time's pinnacle and shout
The battle-cry of truth amid the roar
Of damning multitudes; though curses pour
Their blasting breath upon mine head, and flout
This ragged carcass; though dim spectres rout
The creed of my soul's soul, and to the core
Of my faint heart drive back its frenzied tide;—
Yet the faint music of my last sweet breath
Shall voice my tears, and like an anthem glide
Above the surging threnody of death,
    Till thy dear name my restful lips have sighed,
    And my heart die even while it listeneth.

1888.

FLORIDA.

B Y the stars that circle there
    In and out amid the mist,
By the chill moon's stare,
    And the sea moon-kissed,
Florida, my Italy,
    What a fool you've made of me!

Drowsing sun-steeped by the sea,
    This is how I've found thee waiting
    .   .   .   .   .   .

JANUARY, 1891.

SONG.

L IFE and true love meet but once,
    And though too oft they drift apart,
Yet death alone can fill the void
    Where Love once nestled in the heart.

And lips may smile on sleeping woe,
    And eyes may sparkle through their tears,
Yet who like Memory's self can know
    The phantoms of forgotten years?

A MARTIAL ODE.

"TO arms! To arms!" respondent throats
    Give back the soul-inspiring notes,
  Save mine, which breathes a sigh;
A thousand gleaming falchions shine,
And every lip cries "On!" save mine,
  Which first must say, "Good-by."

"To arms! To arms!" The cohorts stand,
A countless host, a gallant band,
  A stanch and dauntless line;
"To arms!" each man must win or die—
"To arms!" and to their arms they fly,
  And I—I fly to thine!

LOVE IN THE MARKET.

TRIOLET.

THE kiss she threw to Jack,
    Which I chanced by and caught?
'Tis true I gave her back
The kiss she threw to Jack—
Yet was a thief, alack!
    In stealing what he bought—
The kiss she threw to Jack
    Which I chanced by and caught!

SERENADE.

LIFE and I were ill at ease:
  When we were each alone, love,
Time became a slow disease
  With nothing to atone, love,

For the weary hours that pass
  As slowly as a prayer, love,
When the dark cathedral glass
  Stains the outer air, love!

Life and I were friends in name
  Till Life led me to you, love,
And then I saw I was to blame,
  And Life was always true, love!

22

HAMADRYADS.

YE of oak and beechen shades,
  Tender music of the wood,
White of brow, with massy braids
  Coifing gentle virginhood,

Have the cogs and wheels of time
  Dinned upon your coral ears,
With the halting, hum-drum rhyme
  Of these last prosaic years?

Have they tainted that elysian
  Peace and joy ye knew of yore?
Have our eyes imperfect vision,
  That ye are with us no more?

Hamadryads, chaste and coy,
  Ye are still the same, and we,
Mixed and mingled with alloy,
  See not all there is to see!

LOVE'S DIRGE.

WANDERING night-winds passed us, laded
     With the breath of violets;
Mellow moonlight dumbly faded
     Where the water frets
In the wake of tuneful oar,
Like a sighing paramour,
          Dripping, dripping
          Like the tripping
     Music of sweet castanets.

My pale lips on hers had rested
     In the calm of dying pain,
And her sweeping lashes jested
     With a tear or twain;
Still I see the fading vision
Like a smile of sharp derision,
          When one, sleeping,
          Wakes in weeping,
     With the dull-remembered pain.

For I left her, where yon willow
     Drooped and drowsed athwart the stream,
With the rushes for her pillow
     Curtained with a dream.

Yet I cannot but remember
Life's fair June in life's December,
    When no laughter
    Lingers after
All that was, and *is*, a dream!

DESPONDENCE.

FOR the love of a blossom that blew not,
    But paled in the fire of a kiss;
In the kissing of lips that I knew not
The pain of God's wrath I will rue not
    After the ceasing of this!

In the pang of a pain that I know not,
    And tears that I cannot weep
In the paying a debt that I owe not,
I reap the red tares that I sow not
    And sow—as I cannot reap!

1889.

FROM "SONGS OF A PAGAN."

OVER the white sea-foam,
  Into the starlit morn,
Like music through the dome
  That roofs the panting dawn;

Over the dewy hills,
  Into the silent night,
Brushing the daffodils
  In that melodious flight—

Life and Love are fled
  Away on the wild wind's breath,
And they make their bridal bed
  On the blossoming robe of death.

SEWANEE, 1889.

———

HEAVEN may be eternal,
  But it hath no joys for me;
Nor the fire of sunset vernal,
  Nor the pæan of the sea,
Nor the whisper of the ocean
  When time is lost in dreaming,
Nor its scintillating motion
  When the dawn is faintly gleaming.

I have them all, and love them;
  And when my spirit dies,
May it vanish, and be of them,
  And they its Paradise!

———

SEÑORITA, have thine eyes
    No soft glance of love for me,
Nor the music of thy sighs
  Aught that answers mine for thee?

Have thy lips no tender moods
  When they know not what they miss—
When a breaking smile intrudes
  And a smile becomes a kiss?

Señorita, fare thee well!
  "Yo te amo," I would say,
But thy bright eyes look my knell,
  And thy sweet lips say me nay!

27

LOVE, be thy lips the cradle of my sighs,
  Mingling their fragrance with thy sentient
    breath,
Till they are born again in melodies
  And orisons of love, cast at the feet of death.

Love, be thy heart the registry of mine,
  Whose tear-stained tablets may unopened lie,
Until my soul hath bid adieu to thine,
  And all things fade save those which cannot die.

———

MY dream hath fled, and its airy dome
  Hath crumbled into dust, and I,
Like a desolate bird without a home,
  Ask but a spot in which to die.

The holiest shrine of holy love,
  The joy existence held for me,
The light of the stars that smile above,
  My spirit found in thine and thee!

L IPS have smiled till smiles were tears,
　　And eyes have oft grown passing blue,
Yet breathed no echo from the heart—
　　No echo true.

And oft the dewy breath of love
　　To passion's heavy utterance grew,
Yet never hath my thirsty heart
　　Drunk echoes true.

Ye winds asleep upon the sea,
　　Oh! wake ye in a howling crew,
And thunder to the skies a curse
　　That *may* be true!

SEWANEE, 1889.

TO R. B.

STANCH be thy bark
　　When the skies are dark
And the storm's wild wings are free,
　　And the billows leap
　　Where the still sands sleep
On the margin of the sea!
　　And ere we part,
　　From a heavier heart
Here's a health to thy heart and thee!

　　Fair be thy dreams,
　　When waking seems
To live again in sleep,
　　And thine eyes smile o'er
　　A fairer shore
Than that shore on which men weep!
　　So the purple sea
　　Of this health to thee
Be deep as my heart is deep!

Life is but brief,
And time is a thief,
And death hath a master-key
To free the soul
When the jailer's bowl
Is red with revelry;
May thine be true!
With a last adieu
And a health from my heart to thee!

SEWANEE, 1888.

S ORROW'S solution
    Ends with the tomb!
Vaunting ambition—
Vain is its mission,
Lost in the gloom
Of humanity's doom!
Though we may sigh for it,
Though our hearts die for it,
All is in vain!
However we merit,
Others inherit
All but the pain
Of that dreary refrain
Of failing again!
Cease, cease your weeping!
In the still keeping
Of death's chilly eye:
I see a light leaping
In the dull sleeping
Of that which must die,

And, in its purity,
Scorning death's docm!
'Tis the bright surëty
Of that futurity—
Life's retribution,
Sorrow's solution,
Surviving pollution
Born of the tomb!

SONG.

[From "Messalina," an unfinished drama.]

IN a far Greek isle, where the skies were blue,
  And the music of the sea
Haunted the sands where the seaweed grew,
Died in the clouds where the sea-gulls flew,
  And the sun sank wondrously;

In a far Greek isle a little Greek maid
  Walked on the sands by the sea,
Haunted the sands where the seaweed grew,
Gazed into heaven where the sea-gulls flew,
  And the sun sank wondrously.

And the tyrant Cleon saw her there
  With her eyes as deep as the sea,
And the looped-up gold of her circled hair,
And the marblehood of her shoulders, bare
  In the hardihood of sanctity.

And he said, " My child, to be loved of one
  Like thou art, here by the sea,
Would well repay what a god had done
In the sweat of years o'er the wheels of the sun,
  In a nightless eternity!"

34

KISMET.

I SAW her blue eyes quiver
    In the rushes and reeds of time,
Like a naiad's in a river
    Where the hollow waters chime,
Tolled by the winds of even;
    But, oh! she paled and fled—
And the light may be in heaven,
    But the lamp is with the dead!

'Twas music hung about her
    And lingered where she trod;
And Love could do without her
    As faith without a God!
A bud fast shut with showers,
    A wreck of April green,
That dies among the flowers
    To show what should have been.

Her lips were like the water,
    Both passing fair and chill,
As if the sunlight caught her
    And kissed against her will;
Her tongue was lightly laden,
    Her life itself a jest!
The grave hath won the maiden,
    And the daisies tell the rest.

HALIFAX, 1889.

35

WHAT IS LOVE?

TO ——.

HA! what is love? What more than this—
    A pain of soul, an ache of heart;
A sickness of the God in man,
A starving on the Judas kiss
Of flesh and flesh, more bitter than
A poison having no sweet part?
This pain of soul, this ache of heart!
And where was "love" before the soul
Began to knead the well-fit clay?
When Socrates found life to be
The generous path of self-control,
That neither throws God's gifts away
Nor turns them into revelry?

    .   .   .

ONE KISS, AND THEN?

A SONNET.

ONE kiss, and then, like parting wreaths of mist
 That hang in love's red sunset, we grew cold;
 And the last blush of passion-purpled gold
Fell palpitating into amethyst.

One kiss, and oh! the lips that mine have kissed
 Forget, though not forgotten. Shadows fold
 Mine own, and old sweet tales that hers had told
Are but harmonious words without a gist.

Oh! where shall we hang in life's wide eterne,
 When love's white sunrise drives the night away?
What other words upon my lips will burn?
 What other light in her blue eyes will play?
Soft! I have seen a beacon-light afar:
In life's chill night that kiss, love, is a star.

RONDEL.

[A reply to verses in *Harper's Magazine*, October, 1887.]

A SOLUTION.

What Browning meant, the maiden fair
Besought of me in wild despair
 As, seated in a grassy nook,
 We pondered o'er the mystic book
To find the secret written there.

O'erhead the squirrels debonair
Made merry in their leafy lair ;
 Enjoying life, no thought they took
  What Browning meant,

And seemed to say, " You foolish pair,
Be wise, and mystery forswear ;
 Be gay as Doris with her crook
 And Corydon." Then did I look
Up to her eyes, and ceased to care
 What Browning meant.

A WOMAN'S eyes! No wonder, then,
 His Browning was forgotten when
The all outside of Paradise,
Unfathomed still by marvelling men,
 Shone down upon him—Browning-wise—
A woman's eyes!

For man, poor wretch, may search and solve
The rhyme in which the stars revolve,
   Where fire-tracked comets sink and rise,
The liquid spells where gems dissolve,
   Save those whose flash disarms surmise—
   A woman's eyes!

And yet, perhaps, the wise youth saw
What you have guessed not, for one law
   Holds good of things in mystic guise.
"What Browning meant" he found there, for
   All poets they epitomize—
   A woman's eyes!

TO THE ARTIST.

BE silent, emulate the lips of time,
    Upon which silence broods with folded wing
Until it dies within the mighty rush
Of the swift music of triumphant love,
Which bursts upon the world and cries, "Success!"

———

SONNET TO THE SEA.

FOREVER art thou gazing on the sky,
    Forever echoing the stars that pass
    Above thee; now as calm thou art as grass
Ruffled somewhat by spring winds as they fly

Upon flower-robbing wings—and now, the sigh
    Of north-brewed revolution breathes, alas!
    Faints on thy bosom, while a huddled mass
Of thunder-mist is full of ruin's cry.

Yon fern-robed mountain-peak is child of Time,
    And sinks into the dust we sink into,
    The butt of winds in winter's grizzled cope;
Only thine own eternal ebb and flow
Is one, with many changes, like a rhyme
Of many miseries bound about one hope.

40

ODE TO ANACREON.

CHORISTER of love and wine,
    Sweet-tongued rival of the nine,
A double meed of joy be thine!
    Where'er thy sprite hath sought its rest
    In the vineyards of the blest,
Where the leaves are spun of mist,
Trembling o'er the amethyst
    Of bloomy fruit, whose clustered store
    Stains thy silent lips no more—
Revelry and joy be thine!
    Not the revelry of earth,
Where eyes are bright, and hearts repine,
    And woe is cloaked with shrinking mirth;
No such love as fills the heart
    With echoes of what might have been,
Laughing when sweet thoughts depart
    And despair hath entered in;
But the joy and revelry
Which, like buds that blow and die,
    Pales with time and waxeth less
    To bear the seed of perfectness!
Chorister of wine and love,
Such be thine abode above!

SPRING, 1889.

41

FRAGMENTS.

IDEAL WOMAN.

THE possible of woman is to be
The span of God that compasseth mankind;
The morning of man's east; the goiden brew
Of dreams that night drinks, in the quiet west;
The horizon of life's tired mariners;
The verge which hides God from us, and in hiding
Proves him as yonder limits prove the great
World's symmetry, as music proves that death,
Being hushed, is not the end of things that die,
For silence ends in music! . . .

42

SO seize we on the fairest flesh of them,
  Breathing, in passion's primal mightiness,
Our own souls into their transparent clay;
Worshipping fires that we have blown to life
In our abundance.   Then comes weariness,
And we sleep for a time—dream pleasantly—
And feel a swift returning flush of life,
Which is the welcome of our exiled spirit,
Playing no more the part of perfume in
An odorless bud.
                    .   .   .   The weight
And mental bulk of such far-reaching pain,
Less than the hungry gauntness of slow death
That science wrings from wasting maladies,
Laughs at stiff-fingered dogmas and rough creeds
That honor sin with masculinity;
Sin, the hermaphrodite, the double-edged,
The lesser poisoned, and out-edging death
With the false glitter of fair legends writ
Upon an air-keen blade that leaves the imprint
Of man's nobility on the heart's red core.

43

[Fragment of a drama.]

A WOMAN void of better principle,
　　Given quite over to all devilish things,
Cimmerian-souled, and most unpitying;
Merciless, fierce, destructive, murderous,
I know this woman in my soul to be;
And yet she breathes so sweet an atmosphere,
Full of unspecified rich possibles;
An inarticulate witchery of music,
Whose influence generates all beautiful dreams—
Sweet, rare conceptions in regard to her;
And she doth so subject, adopt, and take
A seeming whiteness, purity, innocence,
The tyrannous sovereignty of our better selves,
That perjury is dear-bought martyrdom,
Guilt but a clash of circumstance, and life
But clay-sphered adoration! Is it so?
And yet—ah, God!—a glory of brief flesh—
Beautiful—beautiful! God, how beautiful!
Foul—foul! mark, Atticus, I name her foul—
Devilish! mark, I call her devilish;

44

But, in her vileness, not a thing apart,
A food for controversy, in the touch
Of sexless speculation to be viewed,
As a green-fleshed, glue-eyed astronomer
Watches the ruin of a pleiad, hung
In the constellated chart of God! Me? me!
And if I feel her eyes' warm influence
Fall on me like a rare intoxicant,
Shall I then pause—pause—pause, perchance to fix
The date of their eclipse? to calculate
The durance of their glory? Oh! I am
No saint, as thou art; nor is my heart bound
By tasks, or narrow functions of the flesh,
But, Samson-like, will cease to grind the mill,
Pulling the roof down on good resolution!
Strong am I in my weakness, as the sea,
Swayed—shaped into unconquerable ebb
And flow by the cold beckonings of the moon.
Pity, my Atticus! Condemn me not.

THE SHOWER.

THE spattered gold of the sky is marred
  By a cloud in the zenith; and the flowers
Are pale and dumb, and stand on guard
  To brave the wrath of summer showers,
    Falling like fiercer music in
    A dome of silence and of sin.

The sea is red with molten gold;
  But, ripple by ripple, the pallor creeps,
Till back on its white heart day is rolled
  And the world and the water sleeps.
    And I—lie dumb among the flowers,
    Thinking of life and its summer showers.

            .   .   .   .

A flutter of chill wind passes first,
  A tongueless calm comes after it;
Then a big drop, in some sky-cup nursed
  Till it overflowed its frothy pit,
    Falls on a violet close by me,
    And the blue bud weeps in an ecstasy!
46

STORM.

IN a ruin of gold
  The sky grew cold,
And the waters were leaden gray;
And the spray,
Like a plume
In a spent night's gloom,
Glared white against the day.
And the sea-gulls' scream,
And the ghostly gleam
Of each wing, and its far faint whirr,—
On my heart they fell
Like the name of Hell
On the heart of a murderer!
And the swash—swish—swash
Of the frozen wash
When the helm lay hard-a-lee!
The whimpering wail
Of the beaten sail—
They palsied the heart of me!
And I begged a prayer
From dumb Despair—
Such things her lips disburse,
But she cheated me then,

47

For I cried " Amen"!
To a cold heart-withering curse.

. . . . . . ,

Then it came to pass
That the calm of grass,
Knee-deep and daisy-starred,
Ruffled and riven
By the winds of heaven,
Where the full moon stands on guard,
Fell on the sea—
Fell down on me,
And I shut my weary eyes:
And there came a dream—
And I rockèd on the stream
That flows through Paradise!

. . . .

Now I heard sweet bells,
'Twas the boat on the shells
That lie on the white still shore—
Then the curlew's call
Burst through it all,
And I rose, and dreamed no more!
But the gist of the whole
Is—the calm of soul
God gives to a man in dread;
For the truth was, ten
Of the coast-guard men
Swore an oath that I was dead!

SANITY.

A FRAGMENT.

I TOO am mad,
   If madness is to think athwart the times!
To build one's temporal environments
Of timeless meditation, and to pass
To old age in no age! Men come and go
And know not what they are, nor whence they come,
But measure life by suns and moons and stars,
To fix themselves, and individualize
Their little epoch! Those of finer stuff,
Men who construct a personality
Of light and thought and spirit, men who build
Upon this base and pedestal of clay
The shadow of their own divinity:
The lightning-like vitality of these
Out-wrestles death, and passes on, and fills
The ragged speculations of their day
With a clear deathless pulse that thrills forever!

SPRING.

O SPRING, sweet solacer of wintry woes;
   Brewer of perfumes, odors crystalline,
And golden essences, that through the air
Temper the winds, and gather in the buds,
Close-petalled from the oblivion of night,
To part their love-locked lips, and give them tongues
To whisper to their dewy paramours;—
Young Spring, fair Spring, sweet neophyte of time,
That knows not pale satiety, but still
With self-suffusëd glory, doth defy
The biting inroads of hot summer-winds,
And stays the sun's swift perpendicular beams
From earth's yet tender cheek; young Spring, fare-
   well,
For I am doomed an exile from thy realms,
Like weeping Naso from Cæsarean smiles.
To dare the bitterness of Tomi's coast,
And pen meek madrigals to bear my tears,
And ease the heart of its superfluous load

Of icy agony.   Yet still, oh! still
Linger upon my recollecting lips
In all the kissing whispers of thy joy;
Robbing the base thief, Time, of his delights,
And making memory an Eden, where
The hope of better things doth still indorse
The echo of good things now passed away!
THOMASVILLE, April, 1889.

TO ——.

I'VE seen storms master Heaven, until she'd weep!
    So doth thine anger master thy calm eyes.
I've seen the fluttering gold of morning sweep
The dull dome and the sea;
But when sweet thoughts with all their alchemies
Leave those depths clear to me,
I have no longer any metaphor
To match them with; so, trancëd evermore,
I gaze at thee and dream of Paradise!

I've seen the full waves plumed with pallid foam,—
    So are thy lips, when anger sits on them.
I've seen a sudden shower fall slant, and comb
    The white spray into quietness, gem by gem;
        And so my song to thee
Would fall into a dream upon thine ear.
Mount time's slow wheels--a swifter charioteer
        Than thine ill thought of me!

Tell me to rest my head upon thy knee!
    I have no more to tell thee—all is told.
    I would mine earthliness were deathless gold
For thee to mint joy out of! Yet, perchance
    The thoughts of mine that dwell on my heart's all—
That all which thou art—transmute what is me,
And goldener than morning's stout advance
    Upon night's camp, my soul shall win, or fall!

GOOD-NIGHT.

GOOD-NIGHT! though we be parted quite
  And you forget, and I defy,
Oh! still, when night hath robbed the sight
  Of things that make sweet memories sigh,
  Still dream that I am standing by,
  As though affection could not die:
Still dream that I have said good-night.

Good-night! though true love waxeth chill,
  Yet there is still a fragrance there
Whose sweetness time may never kill;
  A smile of Love's despair
That cometh yet, and ever will.
And so, though dead, 'tis love's sweet right
  To be forever fair—
And bridge the years with that "good-night."

53

WOMEN AND MICE.*

WHAT woman's not a paradox past all believing?

Built up of smiles and tears, of sky and sod!

In every act the thing of all things past conceiving,

A stumbling-block—a link 'twixt man and God!

A *perfect* woman?   Bah! give me well-alloyed metal.

Perfection is, in most, perfection's bane!

Shall I explore a queen-rose, petal by sweet petal?

A worm?   What is a joy worth without pain?

The touch of music when you ring new-minted treasure

Hath half its sweetness of the baser birth!

There is no deep of stars too deep for man to measure

Because he stands upon the sky-scorned earth.

*The above lines were suggested by a discussion as to the fear of mice to which otherwise courageous women are liable, and the poem not having been completed, an explanation of the apparently whimsical title seems necessary.

RATHER MISPLACED.

A	H! what was that tune your tongue ran in?
	That sobbing and palpitant strain—
Like the smell of dead buds, to a man in
	The chill of November's disdain?
I will hold that ubiquitous fan in
	My hand, while you sing it again.

For anything so unexpected,
	Without any " wherefore" or " why,"
Too frail to be rudely dissected,
	Sufficiently lovely to die,
Though it fade and is gone undetected,
	Leaves a void, which we fill with a sigh.

Oh! why should some classical German
	Play the master in music, and curb
Every melody into a sermon?
	What a pity those critics disturb
The sweet hush between acts, to affirm, on
	Their honor, the thing is superb!

And that song you sang, who could look on it
    As too sentimental or slow?
Preferring sonata or sonnet
    To the tender and tremulous flow
Of that perfume in tone?   Out upon it,
    That critics should criticise so!

      .   .   .   .

What? You don't mean to say you've been singing
    An air from Tannhäuser—that flight
Of sweet quavers and semitones, ringing
    The changes on some underlight
Of emotion and feeling?   Well, bringing
    The thing to a climax—Good-night!

THOMASVILLE, GA.

SERENADE.

O MUSIC, tuneful minister of love,
　　Heal the dumb apathy of patient sleep,
And bid her eyelids swell with dreams, and part
Like the famed shell that shuts the modest pearl
From avaricious eyes; bid each pale pearl
Mirror the one who'd wear them on his heart;
Rape her cool lips of honeyed whisperings,
And lay them on the altar of mine ears,
Deaf to all other offerings!　Oh! glide,
Obsequious music, carpeting thy feet
Upon the breathing silence of the night;
Yet wake her not, but seek some oracle,
Inquiry make of drowsiness and dreams,
What thought it was that came, the last　sweet guest
Of that large host, her charitable heart;
Lest even I, or but the thought of me,
Made music in that hallowed atmosphere,
Mayhap sat on her eyes when they were lost
In Lethe　.　.　.　even I might be
The ghost of that which ushered in her dream!

THE SYBARITE.

"The Sybarite affirmed that he could not sleep for lying upon a ruffled rose-leaf."

I GLANCED once from the chambers of delight,
  Through the broad casement that was builded
    there
By drowsy thought, upon a summer's night,
  When fragrance hung too fragrant on the air;
I gazed between the curtains that hung low,
  And woven were of rare and dreamy things
    That come and go,
Like dust of sweet dead flowers that night winds blow
  Into the eyes of sated slumberings.

I saw the weary moon recline athwart
  A cloud of summer's getting, and she gazed
In the arcana of mine eyes, methought,
  Till they grew purple-shot, and dimly glazed
Like windows of dull stained and time-cracked glass;
  And oft the music of a nameless tongue
    That sang "Alas!"
Did pass about mine ears, and then repass,
  All meaningless, like singings over-sung.

58

And then her bosom's hot caress did melt
    Her cloudy couch into a weeping rain
That veiled her from mine eyes; though yet they felt
    That nameless incantation, and the pain
Of something lost, or fading, yet half-seen,
    Some song half-heard, that sinks upon its wings:
        Some wreck of green
That would have been a blossom, had it been
    A thing that could defy its prisonings.

I lay where many roses, plucked apart,
    Tremored knee-deep upon the marble floor,
Amid unfettered melodies that dart
    Through all things fair; and, as the long night wore
Her bosom into paly dawn with dreams,
    The moon still held me in that thrall of mist,
        With lampless gleams
Of shuttered eyes—more fair than fancy deems, —
    And lips that part with kisses yet unkissed.

Then summoned I a youth, amid the throng
    Of liveried ministers that idle were,
And bade him take a lute and lip a song,
    And bugle me a fretted war with care;
And he upon the borders of my bed
    Sank into music's attitude, and then
        Attuned and fed
My spirit with sweet nourishment—blood, bled
    From wounds the world had made, and kissed again.

And lo! his pale brow sank upon the strings,
   And snapped them with the moisture of a sigh;
And faintly came again the stir of wings,
   Filled with the pain of things that cannot die
And yet are not forgotten—still unsought,
   Unsated still with wëird wandering,
       All music-fraught,
Beside the awful Acheron of thought,
   Upon the bleak sad shore of pondering.

And far within a sky of fancy's make
   I felt an unseen moon, amid the mist
That shook with inner radiänce, as shake
   Hot lips that long to kiss and to be kissed;
And I was lost with seeking her, and dank
   With heavy dew that weighed upon mine head;
       And my lips drank
The vaporous springs of many a mouldy bank
   From whose white shine the weary tempests fed.

And when I wept, my tears were changed to clouds
   That clave unto mine eyes, and there o'erhung
Their nakedness, as prayerful pity shrouds
   The pain upon dead lips that have been stung
By what they kissed, yet kiss again and die.
   Mine ears were full of half-heard eloquence,
       Yet knew nor why,
Nor whence had come that sweet thin melody,
   But fed upon the song, without the sense.

And then the mist in which I beat my wings
   Gave chilly birth unto a summer rain,
And I sank with it, as one sinks and sings,
   Whose tongue hath clean forgot his heart's refrain
Nor will remain its aching confidant,
   But sets upon a journey of its own;
        Mad ministrant
Of blasphemy, and sighs that inly pant
   From lips whose music is a monotone.

Ah me! I lay again by him who slept
   Upon his lute in luted slumberings:
And through the curtains came the dawn, and wept
   To see the sum of my vain numberings,
Upon whose many strings no note might pass
   Save the swift climax of a dumb despair
        That sang " Alas!"
The sad sweet tinkle of an empty glass
   Whose wine is spilt upon the sands of care.

Then I among the ruined roses found
   One petal which had paled beneath my heart,
All folded length-and-crosswise, and even bound
   With frost-frayed edges, and I said, " Thou art
Well slumberless, for this shut flower hath bruised
   Thine case into a thing of garnered sighs.
        And so, misused,
Thy heart begot rebellion, and refused
   To harbor Lethe when she sought thine eyes."

'Twas that and only that! I will it so:
  Great things may come of small, and dreams may
      brood
From ruffled love-locks. Be it joy or woe,
  'Tis but the subtle flavor of their food—
Their food, the heart—and mine was nourishment
  Ill-lipped for joy, who bade his brother woe
      Eat discontent,
And fatten upon dreams, until he blent
  With all sweet things that come, and coming, go!

MACON, GA., January 30, 1889.

TO A BUTTERFLY.

BRIGHT pensioner of wormy servitude,
  Freed from thy thrall of silken cerement,
As though a dirge, in some sweet interlude,
  Had burst into melodious merriment;
Thou smile upon the sullen lips of time,
        Thine is a part
Too brief in Earth's long farce for laggard rhyme
  To make a theme of moralizing art;
  And oh! too near, too dear, unto the rhymer's
      heart.

Light thief of pleasure, I could wish thee ill,
  To find so sweet a sympathy of tears;
As one would crush a laughing daffodil
  In fading finger, palsied by the years,
And die in such fair company that death
        Upon the wing
Of some rich dream might pluck the withered breath
  From the faint lips, and hush the chimes that ring
  With time-cracked dusty throat and tuneless rea-
      soning.

Alas! frail child of Spring's young motherhood,
  Thou art ill-flavored nourishment for death:
Rather the rich and summer-ripened food
  Of joy's red lips—and yet, if thy swift breath

Must still confess a ceasing, let there be
     For thy lone bier
Warm-tinted buds in evening revelry,
  And high-piled petals, making odorous cheer
  In death's dim banquet halls when thy pale ghost
    draws near.

Farther among the flowers thy beauties fade,
  Leaving no epitaph of echoes, nor
One memory of glory. Hadst thou stayed,
  Thy fettered joy had sunken into awe,
For lovely things are things most mutable;
     And oh! 'tis death
Whose lips are fixed and frozen, and even full
  Of wormy silence, where the panting breath
  Is hushed, as though for thee the dumb ear lis-
    teneth.

Ah me! Mine eyes play tempter to my tongue!
  My tongue breeds cankered warfare in my heart;
My heart is but a purple song unsung,
  Save in the pathos of a minor part,
Whose sweeter chords are clogged with aching clay:
    And yet, like thee,
I dream within a dome of summer day,
  And lap the milk of buds, until I flee,
  A pilgrim of the eternal, in thy company.

MARCH, 1889.

THE LEGEND OF THE LOTUS FLOWER.

[Published in *Once a Week*.]

I N bloomy thickets where young hyacinths blow,
   Where dreams the dullard bee, even while he
      sips
Hymettean sweetness from the chaliced flow
Of myriad blossoms, where the tall oaks grow
   In mossen dotage, Lotus lay, with lips
That taught each bud an eloquence
It could not echo,—lips whose red suspense
Bent low the listening ear with raptured reverence.

Pale thought and pilgrim fancies wandered o'er
   The blue-veined tracery of lidded eyes;
And whispering sleep bent heavy-kneed before
Her forest couch, and muttered drowsy lore,
   Soft cadences, and far-heard melodies,
Until her lengthy breathing blent
With laggard dreams, in restful measurement
Of droning leaves and flowers that mouthed their
     own content.

5

Then purple-lipped Priapus chanced to pass,
  In quest of some bright-eyed Bacchante; there
He paused in listening quiet, and, alas!
He saw sweet Lotus in the golden grass,
  And kissed her lips again to wakeful care.
She fled to oaken solitudes
Where but the music-throated thrush intrudes
With shrill-tongued reveille and twilight interludes.

But to the tongueless silence of each spot
  Priapus came in wine-begotten wrath;
And when he found her in a weedy plot
Of tangled water-side, where willows blot
  The mottled tracery of woodland path,
Again sweet Lotus fled away:
And through the wave Priapus saw a ray
Of sunny-tinted hair grow dank and muddy-gray.

Oh! where is she? Oh! where hath Lotus fled?
  In what green-lintelled home doth she dream on,
With pale anemone about her head,
Till buds have grown to flowers within her bed,
  And garnered seeds have made their petals wan?
Is there no purple-chaliced tear
In yonder violet-bed, to mark the bier
Of one whose eyes are shut to dream away the
      year?

Oh! there, where waters sleep, sweet Lotus lies,
    And, margining the deep with dimpled breast,
She turns the petalled pathos of her eyes
Toward the infinite; and in the skies
    Her sprite is tented by the wings of rest.
Priapus found Bacchante in the shade
Of mossy caves, and there beside the maid
An amber-hearted amphora was laid.

AN ANSWER TO A PROPOSAL.

THERE'S a little myrtle alley
 Where the birds sing musically,
Answering the forlorn shiver
Of the rushes in the river
Which you see, through trunk and branches,
Flowing on by twenty ranches,
And the blue sky bent above it,
With the blue hills almost of it.
Here her hammock had been swung,
And her small guitar was flung
Like her second self, within it.
Saying: "She has gone a minute
For some knick-knack"—so I waited
Till the gate-hinge creaked and grated,
And she came toward me, singing,
Arms akimbo, sideways swinging,
With a sprig of myrtle netted
 In the spun gold of her tresses.
No Bacchante—satyr-petted,
 Lilting all her heart confesses,

Ever seemed so joy-inspiring!
 No nun, hushed, or saint-fatiguing,
Cold heart's ashes vainly firing
 Had e'er face with such a leaguing
Of all sanctities—yet human
"Prima-facie"—was this woman.

II.

Seeing me, she started,
Singing lips half-parted
Like a shell, but oh! the
Greeting that flows through the
Scarlet orifice is
Scarce the sound of kisses!
Said I, then: "Forever,
Speak the now or never
Of my soul! thine Alpha
And Oméga shall for
Me be final. Sit, then;
Due deliberation
Fits the judge's station;"
And my lips I bit then
Till a tiny trickling
Fell carnation, tickling
Chin and neck a little.
What cared I a tittle,
When the rapt suspense
Of a fine sixth sense
Stood as harp-string tense?

"So," she said, "you love me; well, then,
 I would ask you too a question,
Very easily answered: Tell, then—
 Tell me, after due digestion
Of the query's meaning, would you
 Mean by any chance that merely
You wished to be my husband?   This is
 Something touching me more nearly
Than a thousand idle kisses!
 For I'll be the wife of no man!
Yet I own myself a woman,
 Feeling for you some affection,
 Which would fly if you consented
To be merely the election
 Of a woman."
                      " Be contented
Yet there's still a way."   I said then,
" Hope is not entirely dead then—
Split the difference."
                      So I won her;
God's wide blessing rest upon her!

MOON AND ROCKS.

A SONNET.

OH! tender siren of the star-swept night,
    Eternal shepherdess of unshorn flocks!
The awful void of thy cold sheep-fold mocks
This bleating thought of thine unthought delight.

Thy golden bosom pillowed on the height
    Of yon slow-paling cloud, and thy long locks,
    Cooling the sun-caught fever of these rocks
Where I have fled the world's unkind despite,

Breed bitter discord in the time-built truce
    Of shackled spirit and beleaguered clay,
Whose hot artillery of tears reduce
    That proud melodious citadel, and slay
Its joyous soldiery, that else would march
Like seried stars in thine eternal arch.

MARCH 15, 1890.

ST. AUGUSTINE.

L AND and sea and sky are tongueless;
　　Hear the waters musically
Sigh like love-birds, heard, yet songless,
　　In a myrtle alley!
Earth is wrinkled, old and gray,
　　Scarred and seared by self-dissection;
God himself hath passed away
In tongue-tied creed, and pious fray,
　　And brotherly correction.

'Nita, where the moonbeams fall
　　O'er pale waters musically,
Calling her as love-birds call
　　In yonder myrtle alley—
Gave her word to meet me here,
　　Promised to bring kisses:
Where can 'Nita be then, where?
Or do her light feet fear to dare
　　A night of dreams as this is?

'Nita is all '*Nita* now,—
  Love, all love, in love's each sally,
Witless as a love-bird's vow
  In yonder myrtle alley.
Mighty in her ignorance,
  And wise in very lack of learning,—
God forbid the luckless chance
That ruins sinless circumstance
  With sinful self-discerning!

Go manufacture sin and halter!
  Pay for priests to keep the tally!
God, who made, alone can alter
  Yonder myrtle alley!
Human sins, nine times in ten,
  Were sins alone to those who named them;
And half the world were sinless men,
Until the glorious moment when   .
  The other half reclaimed them.

And 'Nita, dark-eyed 'Nita knows
  Herself no more intrinsically,
Than the love-bird, or a rose
  In a myrtle alley.
So, I love her, and again
  May God forbid that modern learning
Teacheth her to know, and strain
Her heart-strings, searching for the pain
  That comes of self-discerning!

SEPTEMBER 19, 1890.

ERGO SUM.

LINES UPON THE SEASHORE.

THE sea leaps to my feet, and dies
 Like morning dreams in open eyes,
When renovated consciousness
Forgets what sleepless hours confess.
The sky is laden, and the swift
Wind-battered clouds in remnants drift
To catch the sun-beams, gem by gem,
In dying daylight's diadem.
 O God! To be, and not to be!
To live, and feel, and not to think!
 To see all sights that are to see,
 All beauty and all purity,
To disconnect them, link by link,
 Into the dreams that linger on
 The vanguard of oblivion!
And this is what those clouds are; I
 Am but the clod that thinks of them:
Like muddy pools whose ripples dye
Themselves with every depth of sky
 That trembles o'er the brinks of them.

74

Man hath said that God is not,
  Unless he be a Mind, a Soul;
Ψυχή, λόγος—call it what
  You will—to me it is the whole
Circumference of misery,
  Specification of our clay,
This "Ergo Sum," this sad "to be,"
  This power to think!—and so, to say
" I am;"—because I cannot be
  The thing I wish, the thing I dream,
The thing of which I envy thee,
Oh! sea-born mist, and sky-born sea,
Thou pool with lily coronet,
  Thy music, thou eternal stream,
Where, flower-hedged, thy waters fret,
Whose ripple lips are never dumb,
Although they say not " Ergo Sum."

The sun is set, the sky hath met
The waters in that veil of jet
That curtains their communion; I
  Stand ankle-deep and know it not;
For, after all, though ripples die
  Upon the sands, yet is the spot
In some kind held in simple fee
  For those that follow.   Still the why
And wherefore is not known to me.
And yet I think if I could be
A link in God's totality—

Unsheathed of fleshly circumstance,
　　Nor demarcated by the touch
Of knowledge or of ignorance:
　　A total nothing, part of much,
Such as these clouds are, I should then
　　Feel no Promethean impotence,
　　Nor seek the " wherefore" or the " whence"
Of sea and sky, of gods and men;
　　But, like a music which divides
　　And is but one with many sides
In interlinking harmony,
　　Although I could not think, and sigh,
And feel, and think I could not be,
Yet I should know unconsciously
　　That many, many-tongued reply
　　Which solveth man's coeval " why!"

1890.

THE GLOW-WORM.

THINK you we are what we think we are
       In the clay?
Can a glow-worm think himself a star,
       As they say?
Seeing his own shadow still a worm
       In his glow,
Watching his long shadow twist and squirm,
       Can he know
'Tis his own light shadows forth his clay
       In the night?
Pointing out his lean and wormy way?
       His own light?
Knew he this, would he be wormy still?
       Squirm and twist?
Knew we this, would life still lead up hill
       In the mist?
Knew we this, would strength fail in our need?
       Soul bear scars?
Is the worm's fire not the self-same breed
       As the star's?

DECEMBER 15, 1890.

NIGHT.

NOW the white hollow of the day's spread wings
    Sinks rippling into darkness, and is gone!

    .   .   .   .   .

The long night's brooding calm oppresses me.
The ache of no sound, and the moon's cold white;
The blanched earth and the sky hung over it,
Swelling with thunder and quite bare of stars;
Communion of dumb trees and shuddering winds;
The frozen baldness of cathedral spires;
The cold sea, baring cheek and bosom to
The dead moon, and, for love of her faint kiss,
Still shoreward stumbling in the dark forever!

    .   .   .   .   .   .

TO A LIVING PREACHER OF INFIDELITY.

TO be a rebel is a noble thing;
   But thou art but a slave, who loves his chains,
Nor knows the name of freedom, yet would fling
   His envious sneer upon all that disdains
His foul corruption. Thou wouldst plant thy sting
   And sully with thy heart's corroding stains
   All things that are yet fair, to glory in thy pains.

Hath yonder purpling ocean no mute prayer
   For hearts like thine? Can thy polluted eyes
Count the bright stars, the high, the darkly fair,
   And lie unto thy lips, till they despise
That which they cannot lisp? Alas! despair
   Must teach thy heart the lesson it defies,
   And sing thy tuneless ear a pæan from the skies.

Oh! tell us, Glory, who hath made thy creed,
   Which countless lips count o'er in pale unrest,
While the frail heart's vain hope and longing feed
   The worm *thou* hast engendered; what vain jest
Tempts thee to deck the dull and soulless weed

With honor's trappings and a gaudy crest,
While many a violet dies unseen in some green
nest?

.   .   .   .

Alas! how hast thou made a sport of one
Who cannot see the path his footsteps tread,
But staggers on till his brief day is done,
With piteous mirth—from his own weakness fed—
Upon those lips whose laughter cannot shun
The shadow of the end, where all are led
To take a nameless place among the nameless dead!

80

THE UNSEEN SINGER.

BY all my soul must be
   When death devours me,
Worn limb from limb and weary bone from bone,
   I never dreamed or thought
   That all the music taught
By God to clay could equal thine alone!

   Lost there among the leaves,
   Like some mad thought that heaves
The coils and knotted tangles of the brain,
   The fire of thine intense
   Life conquers soul and sense,
Until to see thee singing were a pain;

   To see, and so to crush
   Imagination's rush
Of dreams that bear thee starward through the night;
   To see, and so to say:
   "God writes a psalm in clay!"
For faith in God himself would die at sight!

But when the air's a-tremble
With singings that assemble
All shapeless ecstasies and visions vain,
The sweep of our own wings,
In seeking him that sings,
Makes angels of us in doubt's passing pain!

And so thou art a type
Of God, whose song is ripe
For all men, and, to find the singer, we
Have risen from the mire,
Are what we are, and higher
Must wander on, until we cease to be!

For if the clearest eyes
That ever read the skies
In fullest vision pictured God to men,
The end of things would be:
The mire cries "man" for me
When doubts are solved and peace hath come again.

This peace and death are one—
This longing after none
Of those impossibles that hang above
The utmost grasp of us—
The fruit of Tantalus,
Whose swaying shadow is our faith and love!

Thou dost not sing such peace!
That sinking and increase—
That silence now, that rush of music then—
Are not the drowsy flow
Of lips that murmur " Go,
Disturb us not, we wish to sleep again!"

So joy and sadness both,
Though sadness something loath,
Are mates for life whose mad hopes never cease;
But God, whose glory dies
Each evening in the skies—
'Tis He alone that is, and must be, Peace.

JANUARY, 1891.

THE SUICIDE.

In ancient Mexico it was the custom to gratify every whim
and caprice of a living sacrifice during the year previous to
his immolation.

YE whose fair task it is to spill my blood,
    To make this clay a wormy legacy
Unto the future, hear me for a space;
For in the year ye gave me to grow fat
In idleness and kisses, I have learned
Much wisdom and more patience. On the whole,
The death ye grant is all that I could be
Still curiöus concerning—most cold death,
Most clotted, wormy, macerated death—
The thing I know not—I, whose cheek is warm
With fever; I, whose eyes were ever wont
To emulate that poor unstable star
Whose every breath is brightly changeable!

If ye remember, for the first two moons
I asked for music, wine, and dancing-girls;
Loose-tongued companions, who made wings for
        time,
That could not lift his great unwieldy bulk

From my crushed head and heart.   Lo! sleep forsook
My eyes, and then 'twas, first, I thought of death.
I paced upon the earth-commanding brow
Of yon great temple, till I saw the dawn
Grow broader, like a smile upon the lips
Of some loved woman; and the pale shy stars
Were veiled and interknitted by their own
Slow golden overflow; and all was still
In an unbreathing silence, as though death
Had hushed the haunting echoes of the day,
And himself slept in his own dreamlessness.
And there I shook the breath of wine from me,
The kisses and love-tales that rotted in
My fore-doomed heart; and when the sun arose
I slept like one that hath been cast ashore
On the warm golden sands to find a couch—
And peace unutterable.   From that time
I've dwelt within the vast and shadowed depths
Of forest-deserts; and men think me mad,
One whom anticipation weighed upon,
For whom dreams made sleep madness, till the brain
Awoke no more; and partly they were right:
For who hath smiled on death, as I do now,
Nor thought with other men. . . . Lo! I am mad,
If madness is to think athwart the time;
To build one's temporal environments
Of timeless meditation and to pass
To old age in no age!

Men come and go
And think not whence they come, nor where they go:
But measure time by the sun, moon, and stars,
To know themselves, and individualize
Their little epoch.   Men of finer stuff—
Men who construct a personality
Of light and thought and spirit; men who build
Upon this base and pedestal of clay
A fiery statue of their own intense
And lightning-like vitality—'tis these
Whose pulsing life out-wrestles death, and passes
Into that newer tenement, and fills
Its fibrous speculation with a fire
That burns forever.
                            Ye who walk upon
The path your fathers trod, and see no deep
And awful vistas stretched upon each side
Unto the dim horizon which is God—
Ye find a grave dug at the farther end,
And there ye stop, and sleep, and feed young worms
That live as ye have lived, to green old age,
And die as ye will die.   Yet ye set up
A god to serve who serveth also you,
Bends to your lips to catch the impure breath
That floats in poisonous vapors from the earth
And breeds night-gendered fungi, and soft toads,
Slime-vestured types of twice ten thousand prayers;
And from the tongue of this divinity

Ye draw eternal life, as I would pluck
A reed, and breathe into its hollow heart
And find the music I was fondest of—
Be it a hymn or drinking-song!

                    What say ye,
The time is come for sacrifice?

                         Well, well!
Stay, while I look once more upon the sky,
So charactered and so unreadable,
So full of music and sweet tongueless sounds,
So full of perfume, when the summer-winds
Drink the buds dry.   Stay, while I gaze again
Upon my refuge:—the quiet assemblages
Of mossy-bearded centenarians,
That seem to take me with their long green arms
And call me to the feet of them, to lie
And dream sweet things among the berried shrubs
That slipper their worn feet.   Of such a shrub,
That which hangs low with purple treasury
Of lush large berries, I did eat my fill,
Pressing their bursting forms upon my tongue
And sucking out the bitter juice of them,
And saying: Death, if thou canst lurk within
Full-fleshed vitality; if thou art thus
A guest in the whispering hostelry of life;
There is in thee some music which we hear not,
Some sweet potentiälity of that
Which is not desolation and despair.

I find no poison in so fair a dish
Upon God's table—so I sup with Him,
And He is host; and I thus bow to Him—
And—ye are fading from me. . . .

                        Pull that rug
To my numb feet, that I may rest a space,
For I can look upon the sun unblinded—
So dim mine eyes are!

                 Are ye ready, then?
I also . . . but go with you—not to-day.

MEMORIES.

A STUDY IN E MINOR.

HEAVENS!   Do you call *this* Easter-love, when
the air
Hangs leaden-like with perfume?   When the sky
Gathers her flock of moon-deserted stars
Into a haze of golden ether?
                              Listen!
That faint full monotone of breakers, dying
In sighs upon the beach——

   .   .   .   .

                   The laughing leap
Of little star-lit waves upon the feet
Of Marco's battlements, *these* second me
And cry "Amen" to my poor lip-worn prayer.
Forget the unlovely resolution which
Lurks like a baffling lump of poison in
Thy life's full cup!   Oh, be a child of all
The years that have been and are yet to be!
To crown eternity with love—this is
Thy mission, and the convent yonder,

Where the star-echoes sleep like children dreaming
Upon the cool dome of a spring-dug grave,
Is full of bones that never knew the flesh,
Yet might have been as fair as thou art now,
With summer in the cheek, the quickening essence
Of night in their deep eyes, and music in
The very sighs of them, as sweet as that
Which seemeth like assent upon thy lips,
Now, even now! . . .

       That " yes" means life to me,
And love, and . . .

       Hush! What mellow choir is there?
The hymn? Ah! yes, the Easter hymn . . . and
    listen
How the notes blend, as if an alchemy
Made the poor dross of many tongues and hearts
A golden unity of music! What?
Weeping? Yes, I too feel the tears in that
"Santa Maria," and the rest of it;
A fallacy, sung on a night like this,
Hath more conviction in it than the muttered
Truths of . . .

       What? You say "farewell" to me?
And a few harmonics have blotted out
That "yes" of thine? the misbegotten child
Of love and reason?

       Go, then—leave me here
Like some foul toad that sits among the fens

And brews green poison! Seek some butterfly
As thou art, sick with honey that ferments
In every summer air that breathes on it!
    .   .   .   .

O God! That music hath o'er-brimmed mine eyes,
Yet is but music . . . and I am alone.

MARCO MIALE.

M ARCO MIALE—cardinal—stood forth,
    Hushing the mingled voices with "Amen!"
To-day's long task is finished, for the sun
Rims the dim west with glory. Hush! one—two—
There's the boom . . . boom . . . of the Angelus!
                              Enough
Of whys and wherefores, and that matter of
The new-built monastery, nestling far
Among the purple Euganéan hills—
And still unpaid for; God's time is not ours.
See, Matteo lays the board, there, where the rock
Bears that alcove above the pine-tree tops.
Look at the broad blue shadows of the night
Resting among the vineyards! Those white spots
Are dwelling-places, and that darker patch
Is a broad field of uncut grain; but there,
Away there, where the blue-black hills shoot up
Into the golden sky—I see the lake,
Bearing the last slant shaft of fire that breaks
The mist through . . and, d'ye know, I've seen a
    soul
Not unlike this. First, its totality

Was God—just as the unseen all of this
Is the whole world. Then there were mists that
    hung
Over its fields of cut and uncut grain;
And then death came, as night comes to us now,
Moulding the stiffening lips into a smile.

 . . . . . .

Too curiöus, I fear, too curiöus—
What is't to you what thoughts I thought, or where
I wandered? Yet, sit nearer, and the tale
Shall, as you wish, be told you, then. A woman?
A woman, say you? Ay, it was a woman!
And yet why should I trust the thing to you,
To whom, as soldier of our God, that love
I think of is an alien?
       I? Hear, then.
Priest as I am, I felt, and did not die!
Then my lips clinched in some fierce sense of fear,
And far beneath me in unmeasured depths
A faint light broke, like music, palpitant.
You are well out of it, for this same love
Is neither of the spirit nor the flesh,
Yet hath an edge for either; and the day,
In the white hush of noontide, or when night
Plays with the slow feet of the twilight—night,
Checked by the moon's mild fire, and full of music
Such as the leaves make when the winds pass by—
Both cease to be in love's fierce period;

Both premises to one conclusion—
In my case being negative—and that
Necessitates, you recollect, despair!

Since Christ died, fifteen hundred and two score,
'Twas then she died, too, and I cried " Amen!"
Folded my hands, and now am cardinal.
                                    We'll sup
With the last sunlight shooting through the wine;
And that brings back to me a matter heard
Long, long ago in fanciful Provence,
The fruit of a woman's lips, that sank in the end
From riddles into music.   Thus it was . . .

        .   .   .   .   .

There was a little balcony that hung
In the great quiet night over the moonlit sea,
And she came there for solitude, and brought
Her lute along, and as she sat she sang;
And he half caught the music, and approached
Unthinkingly, not knowing who it was;
And thus the words came throbbingly to him:

        There is a dead hope in my heart,
            Like a dead star in the sky.
        "God's light falls on it day by day;
        Thank God there's a star in Heaven," men say,
            " Whose fires will never die!"
        And it makes me weep, for the thing is dead,
        And men's praise is but gall to me;

94

And yet God's light is better by far
Than the burned-out fires of that dull dead star.

.   .   .   .   .   .

Quoth Bishop Rizzio, "I do cry Amen
To your conclusions.   Faithfully have you,
My brother, caught the fire of Sinai!"
"Well, are you weary?   Yet one question still
I ask you, as in sport, to make you smile,
And give a sweet taste to your dreams to-night.
What single portion of our corporal being,
The earthly sheath of our divinity,
Say you, hath been the firmest true support,
The instrument and ally of ourselves,
The path-constructor to eternal rest?
"This," cried Carola, "this firm hand of mine,
Which like a greater Atlas doth hold up
A greater world, in bearing God's sweet flesh
In reverent sacrament!"
                              And Maffio cried:
"Amen! well spoken.   Yet this tongue of mine,
Swaying the mighty masses, as the moon
Calls to the stubborn sea-waves, hath it not
Gained my poor soul a better surëty
Of life than fleshly functioner can give?"

And Timon cried: "Thy tongue is eloquent,
O Maffio, consigning to God's service
The honey of old Hybla; yet these feet,

Scarred by the flints of Palestine, have thrice
Borne me to God's sweet sepulchre, and so
Thrice borne me nearer God's three-seated throne!"

Cried Rizzio, in conclusion unto them:
"My dim and tattered eyes have borne me thrice
Three thousand times to God in His sweet book;
And though I lose hands, feet, and tongue, yet I
Knock louder than you all at His shut door,
Out-bristling lions in my confidence,
My eyes the barristers in my defence!"

"Well! well!" they cried, and so there came a pause.
"Ho, there!" cried Maffio to an ancient monk,
Whose task it was to heap upon the board
The evening meal. His was no sinecure
In life's allotments, and he had grown old,
And had become no wiser. "So," cried Maffio,
"And you, good brother! Say you, hands or feet,
Dim eyes or palsied tongue, have guided you
Nearer to God, and made you confident?"
And he was quick abashed at the demand
From so much purple-plushed magnificence;
So his old tongue refused to favor him
Till Maffio cried: "Speak, dotard!"
                                    When he spoke,

And answered:
"Please your reverence, my knees.'

CLEON, the sculptor, stood, one arm about
  The shoulders of his daughter Cynthia,
One weary elbow resting on a block
Of jagged marble, while upon his hand
Leant his white brow, whose wrinkled charactry
Spelt out the epitaph of youth and joy.
She was the full-kept promise of his love;
Her red lips lending eloquence to words
More harsh than heavy discord, and her eyes
Indorsing each sweet promise of her lips,
Too bright in their own matter to be dimmed
By trifling comparison of stars,
Too dark in their own night to be out-nighted
By the most ebon moodiness of night,
When she hath bid the moon go hide herself
In some dank dungeon of unwholesome mists.
" Thou art not like thyself, my father! Say
What canker-worm hath fed upon thy peace?
What caitiff thought hath been the self-made guest
Of thy too hospitable heart, and turned
Upon its host with cold ingratitude?"

"Alas!" said Cleon, "this same stubborn stone
Hath locked that thought within its milky keep!
For young Timoleon, that youth who lives
To seek coy wisdom, burning out his eyes
Like flickering torches in the bootless search,
Timoleon hath commissioned me to carve
A statue of that thing which he calls 'truth;'
Hath given direction that this Truth shall be
In likeness of a long-interrèd corpse,
With worm-entunnelled eyes, and smiling jaws
That smile, in that they lack their silent lips
To smile with. Further, that the pedestal
Be skulls, piled up into a pyramid:
And yonder stands the pedestal of skulls,
Beneath the silk deceit of that pale curtain,
That droops in long sad folds, as if to weep
Its sickly office.
                    But this stone
Doth still refuse the manufacturing
Of that which is to be erected there;
Yet young Timoleon hath builded him
A subterranean study, marble-roofed,
And hung with sweet medicinable lamps,
Where solitude doth make a silent third
To wisdom and her sateless neophyte;
And there he purposes to place the thing
To be presiding spirit, sweet familiar
To his most sad, lugubrious visiöns."

"Sweet father, I have been thine only child,
And so thrown much with thee in my brief years
Of meted time; and thus I do profess
Limited skill of some sort in thine art,
Got more from observation than aught else;
Give *me*, then, the commission of this task,
And I will lay a wager with old Death
That I will work more grisly work than he,
And he give up his trade in sheer despite!
For I will cut the marble into shape
At which the frighted chisel will grow dull,
And be unwilling minister to hands
That force it to so chill a task!"

                                        "So be it!
For my part," said old Cleon, "I have done
With this phantasmagoria of death—
And for the long space of a year will I
Conquer no form but leaping water-nymph
And smiling hamadryad! So, farewell
To Truth, if Truth be such as he hath said."
"Then tell Timoleon," said sweet Cynthia,
"That on the morrow, in his quiet nest,
Wilt thou set up his scare-crow Truth, to fright
Henceforth all tender falsehoods and gilt lies
From his sweet harvest of acquirements."
"What, by to-morrow even?"

                                    "Ay," she replies.
"To limn out Beauty's soft seductiveness

Might take a longer time, but to give form
To some foul nightmare such as all have felt
In sleep-distorted moments, what is that
But recklessness of finer tone and touch?
As one would dash a passion-driven hand
Upon a harp's responsive strings, and wake
A fiend in that bright Paradise of sounds,
Make discord of sweet possibilities,
And blow up war in Music's brotherhood!"

Timoleon, on the morrow, took his way
To his new dwelling, as the sun went down,
Stripping of all their purple uniform
His soldiery of clouds, until they looked
Quite woe-begone, like self-stung renegades
That had gone over to advancing night.
Timoleon's brow was shaded o'er with cares
Which hung like murky mists upon the face
Of some fair mountain-pool, and his damp locks
Lay mutinously heaped upon his head,
Save one or two, which fell about his eyes
Like long rich grasses o'er twin springs of thought,
Peering into their calm transparency,
And ruffling that calmness with a kiss.

In the quiet midst of self-reposing gloom
Stood the pale mimic of deceiving Truth.
Sweet Cynthia herself stood, pedestalled

By skulls, and thereby seemed more softly fair,
In the stern concord of antithesis.
For she did nourish love of this poor child
Who cried out for a bauble; knowing not
That love of wide-spread popularity,
To be the theme for gaping in a crowd,
Is oft mistook for most divine resolve;
And so doth pave the highway unto hell,
Upon whose every stone is writ " I will,"
Until the multiplied affirmative
Hath negatived itself and damned the speaker.

Timoleon stood, as though in mimicry
Of purblind ignorance, who comes upon
The thing he sought, and knows it not; then said:
" Ha! Cleon hath mistook my drift most sadly—
For this poor manufacture of his brain
Hath more the posture and self-confidence
Of sophistry,—that pretty cloak of lies;
And, in the very climax of deceit,
He hath here wedded color unto form,
And stained the virgin marble with a taint
Of worm-predestined nature. Oh! alas!
Scale off the painted richness of a cheek—
What have we but the very commonplace
Of dust and creaking sinews, that grow stiff
And weary of their several tasks so soon?
Tear off the alleviäting tapestry

That doth hang o'er the eyes—what have we then
But staring pupils in a sea of white,
Looking like some sweet fruit that hath been plucked
From its o'er-sheltering leaves, and hung aloft
In bald desertion?   All things so deceive us?"
" 'Tis thou that art deceived," cried Cynthia,
" Because lush damask lies upon a cheek—
Yet knewest me not—but bone doth lie beneath.
Oh! are the myriad pearly diadems
That lie within the shine of yonder sea
To be spread out in auction to thine eyes,
Because thou hast cried 'liar ' to the sea?
Poor worm, that hath mistook its daily food,
Feeding on bitter aloes, till all things
Did sting its palate with the memory
Of its diurnal nourishment!   Poor toad
That hath sucked poison in its native fens,
Until the stars stagnate within their spheres
To his foul hornèd eyes! "

                             " Sweet lecturer! "
Cried out Timoleon, "were I a toad
I had not thought thee but a marble dream!
Were I a worm, I'd lay me at thy feet,
And starve upon the chances of thy death,
To feast upon thy treasures!   As I am,
I can but offer thee a pupil who
Hath learnt his lesson, and but asks thy leave
To tell it in thine ear.

Sit we upon
These skulls, that love therefore be sweeter yet
Upon so sour a camping-place.   Just so.
Wilt thou then be addition to my creed,
Changing in that addition all before?
Yet say not in gross words, that ill conform
With these most silent witnesses, but turn,
As they to one another—be our eyes
Commissioners to make that treaty good
Of which my lips make purport unto thine.
So yield thee, while I flatter these poor arms
That they at last have grasped and circled Truth."
    1889.

FAREWELL VERSES.

TO ———.

OH! would that we could pierce the gloom
    That clouds the pathway to the tomb,
And mark the course our feet must tread
Before they rest among the dead;
And where we smile, and where we weep;
And where we dream, in waking sleep,
Before we sleep upon the shore
Where slumberers dream and wake no more!
Alas! from life's storm-beaten crest
We fix our eyes upon the west,
Where our own sun must one day set,
Though pausing in the zenith yet,
But see no path amid the mist,
No shore by distant ocean kissed;
No limit to that mortal thing
Whose hourly knell our heart-beats ring;
No silence for that whispered song
Whose music cannot whisper long;

No rest for that, whose restless sigh
Proclaims it but a thing to die.
Yet there is still an echo borne,
And still we catch a note forlorn—
A whisper from that lone retreat
Where darkling shore and ocean meet;
And in red revelry and rout,
When hearts have shut remembrance out,
And souls have sought the loved caress
Of one brief hour's forgetfulness,
'Tis then, when we have turned our eyes
From where the past in ashes lies,
That cheeks are clammy with the spray
That dashes palsied time away,
And curls about the panting heart.

My friend, all human souls must part;
The echo of our being's knell
Is borne upon that word " Farewell."
But, as the ocean glimmers yet
When yonder paling moon hath set,
And as the clouds still blush with day,
Though twilight long hath passed away;
So love and friendship, though they die
Yet live, if there be but one sigh
To catch the light still feebly shed,
And bear the impress of the dead.
I too have felt ambition's sting

When crushed by her enfeebled wing;
Yet, tempted still, with eagle eye
She searches glory's fading sky,
And marks the star she cannot gain—
Then dies but to be born again.
I too have breathed the galling sigh
Of time-enshackled misery,
And felt my spirit many a day
Half turn within its grave of clay,
And, maddened by the numbëd pain,
Fall fainting into sleep again!

Yet, ——, when we say farewell,
'Tis mine, and mine alone to tell
To *sorrow's* ear my loss; to thee
The meed of human prophecy.
Thy foot is where mine cannot stand,
Upon no shifting path of sand,
Nor wandering on the treacherous shore
Of that which thou can'st ne'er bridge o'er.
Thy faith is what mine cannot be.
Thy spirit in its sphere is free.
Rebellious curses cannot blight
Thy lips, nor dark despair alight
Upon the temple of thy creed.

My friend, may thy stanch spirit speed
Thy footsteps on, and like a star

Whose silvered breath is borne out far,
May that success which breathes in thee
Bear thy reflected light to me,
And write, like old Belshazzar's doom,
A " Pax Vobiscum" on my tomb!

SEWANEE, 1888.

APPENDIX.

FAREWELL ADDRESS TO AN OLD COATEE.*

[Written for Undergraduates' Day, '87, University of the South, Sewanee, Tenn.]

FAREWELL, Old Coat, farewell forever,
  And yet 'tis hard that we must part;
For we've been comrades long together,
  Breast to breast, and heart to heart.

We have braved, all uncomplaining,
  Summer sun and wintry blast;
Now, Old Coat, thy star is waning,
  And we two must part at last.

With glory thou wast once invested;
  So, old friend, it might be still,
Had not we two marched together
  Many an hour of "extra drill."

* This poem, immature as it is, finds a fitting place in an appendix because of its association with the poet's Alma Mater, and the warm requests of many of his college friends to have it put in print.—ED.

There, Old Coat, 'twas first we quarrelled,
  The sun was hot, you recollect;
And I used some strong expressions
  That hurt your pride and self-respect.

So you made it hotter for me,
  And when the extra drill was o'er,
I tore thee off, old friend, and threw thee
  In the dust upon the floor.

But we made it up, old comrade,
  At the next " Battalion Hop,"
Where all night we danced together,
  Till morning forced us both to stop.

And fair hands lay on thy shoulder
  Just where the rusty rifle lay;
With such "arms" as that, old comrade,
  We'd march "extras" every day!

And we tripped a "double quick,"
  Lightly to " Blue Danube's River;"
Then we marched at "common time,"
  Out where the silvery moonbeams quiver.

We have many a recollection,
  You of me and I of you;
But we've promised to each other
  To be silent friends and true.

"Gown" will never sit as lightly
  As thou hast in days gone by;
Dreams of glory with thee perish,
  Bright illusions with thee die.

Sell thee, comrade? Sell thee? Never!
  Thou art scarcely worth a V;
While thou hast sweet recollections,
  Tender memories for me.

So, Old Coat, farewell forever!
  We must bow to destiny;
Like true friends we've served together,
  Like true friends we'll say good-by.

And I'll place thee in some corner,
  Safe from iconoclastic eye,
Where thou canst count the dust of ages
  In oblivion's sanctity.

Thou shall be a fitting pillow,
  Where memories of the past may sleep;
Where the ghosts of by-gone "extras"
  At midnight hour may wake and weep.

We have scarce a moment left us,
  My heart, old comrade, throbs thy knell;
And thine, I know, is breaking also,
  Taps are sounding—Fare thee well!

www.ingramcontent.com/pod-product-compliance
Lightning Source LLC
Chambersburg PA
CBHW022144020726
47496CB00008B/2547